Animals

Baby ELEPHANTS

JUSTIN ERIC RUSSELL

WORLD BOOK

This World Book edition of *Baby Elephants*
is published by agreement between
Black Rabbit Books and World Book, Inc.
© 2020 Black Rabbit Books,
2140 Howard Dr. West,
North Mankato, MN 56003 U.S.A.
World Book, Inc.,
180 North LaSalle St., Suite 900,
Chicago, IL 60601 U.S.A.

Marysa Storm, editor; Catherine Cates, interior designer;
Grant Gould, cover designer; Omay Ayres, photo researcher

Library of Congress Control Number: 2018025963

ISBN: 978-0-7166-3902-2

Printed in the United States of America. 1/19

BOLT

Image Credits
Alamy: Simon Eeman, 19
(btm); iStock: cinoby, 13 (btm);
jacus, 22–23; PeterBetts, 28; Shutterstock:
abxyz, 31; Andre Klopper, 27 (newborn silhouette); Claire E Carter, 6; Edwin Butter, 4–5;
Four Oaks, 6–7; Gregory Zamell, 25; gualtiero
boffi, 27 (adult silhouette); Gunter Nuyts, 19 (top);
Johann Marais, 8; Johan Swanepoel, 3, 32; John Michael Vosloo, 16; Kirill Trubitsyn, 13 (top); Manekina
Serafima, 14–15; Michael Potter11, 27 (top); Nattaya
Maneekhot, 24; paula french, 1; SouWest Photog-
raphy, 20; Steve Bower, Cover; THRUS PANYAWA-
CHIROPAS, 10–11
Every effort has been made to contact copy-
right holders for material reproduced
in this book. Any omissions will be
rectified in subsequent printings
if notice is given to
the publisher.

Contents

CHAPTER 1

A Cute and Playful

A baby elephant seeks shade from the hot sun beneath its mother. It fans itself with its floppy ears. Soon, more elephants arrive. They hug the baby with their long trunks. The group leads the baby to a river. The little elephant splashes in the cool water. Ahh!

First Steps

Baby elephants, called calves, are playful. Within half an hour after birth, they can stand. They soon take their first steps. Calves are wobbly at first. But with help from their families, they soon get their balance.

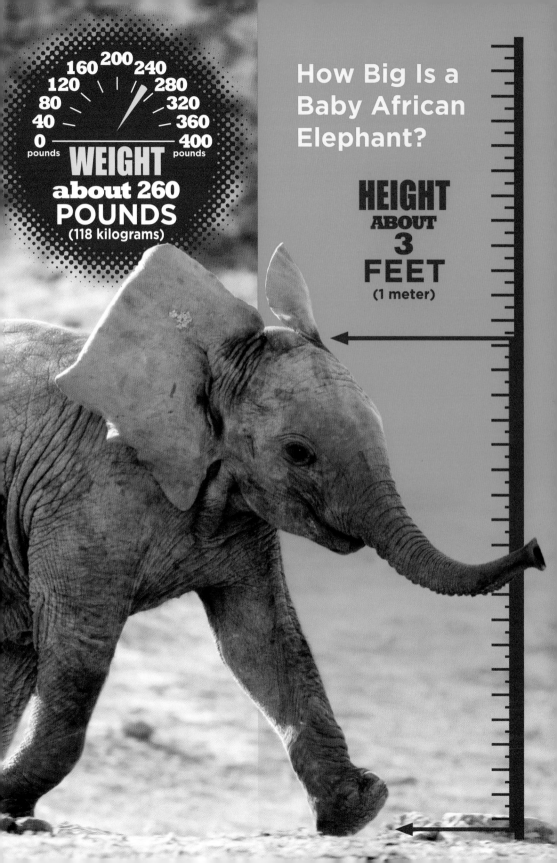

WEIGHT
160 200 240
120 280
80 320
40 360
0 400
pounds pounds

WEIGHT
about 260
POUNDS
(118 kilograms)

How Big Is a
Baby African
Elephant?

HEIGHT
ABOUT
3
FEET
(1 meter)

Elephants use their trunks to feel, push, and pull things. Trunks also help them drink. Elephants use them to suck up water and pour it in their mouths

A Mighty Nose

Baby elephants stick close to their families. They have a lot to learn, such as how to use their trunks. Newborns are **clumsy** with their trunks. It takes calves months to learn how to use them.

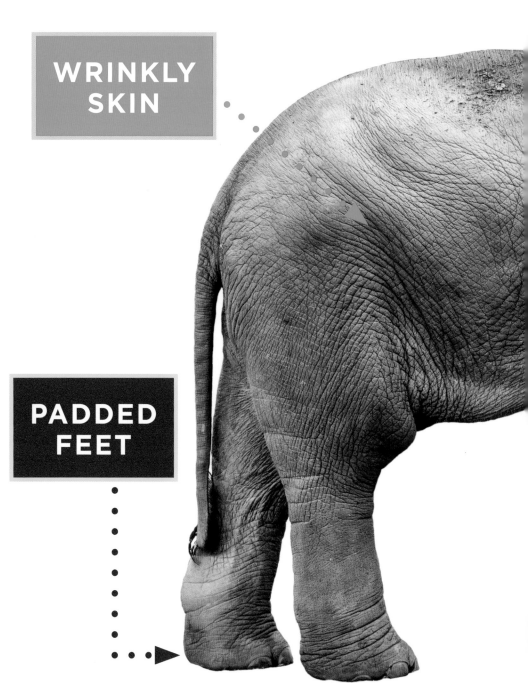

BABY ELEPHANT FEATURES

WRINKLY SKIN

PADDED FEET

LARGE EARS

EYES

TRUNK

STURDY LEGS

CHAPTER 2

A Place to Call

There are two types of elephants.
African elephants live in African
forests, grasslands, and deserts. Some
make their homes in rain forests too.
Asian elephants live in Asia. They can
be found in rain forests and
along rivers.

AFRICAN ELEPHANTS

ASIAN ELEPHANTS

Elephants communicate using their trunks.

Family and Friends

Elephants are **social** animals. Females and their young live in groups. These herds can have just a few to more than 100 elephants. An old, **experienced** female leads each group. It leads the elephants to food, water, and shelter. All group members help take care of calves.

Playtime

Baby elephants play with other calves in the herd. They chase and push each other. Playtime is training for baby elephants. They learn to keep their balance and use their trunks. Playing also teaches them social skills.

Herds protect baby elephants from **predators**. When an elephant senses danger, it trumpets. Adult elephants then form a protective circle around the calves.

CHAPTER 3

WHAT'S FOR DINNER?

Calves' first meals are their mothers' milk. They **nurse** for their first few months. At four months old, most calves can eat solid food. They still nurse, though. Once they're two to three years old, they eat only solids.

Adult elephants spend about 16 hours each day eating.

Finding Food

Adult elephants mostly eat grass, leaves, bark, and roots. They also enjoy fruits on tall growing trees. They feed during the early morning and late evening. Young elephants learn what to eat by watching the adults.

Adult African elephants eat up to about 300 pounds (136 kg) of food daily.

BY THE NUMBERS

1

NUMBER OF YOUNG FEMALE ELEPHANTS HAVE AT A TIME

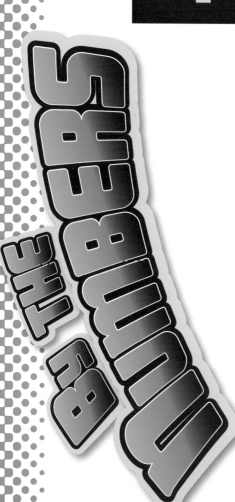

20 to 22 MONTHS

how long female elephants are pregnant

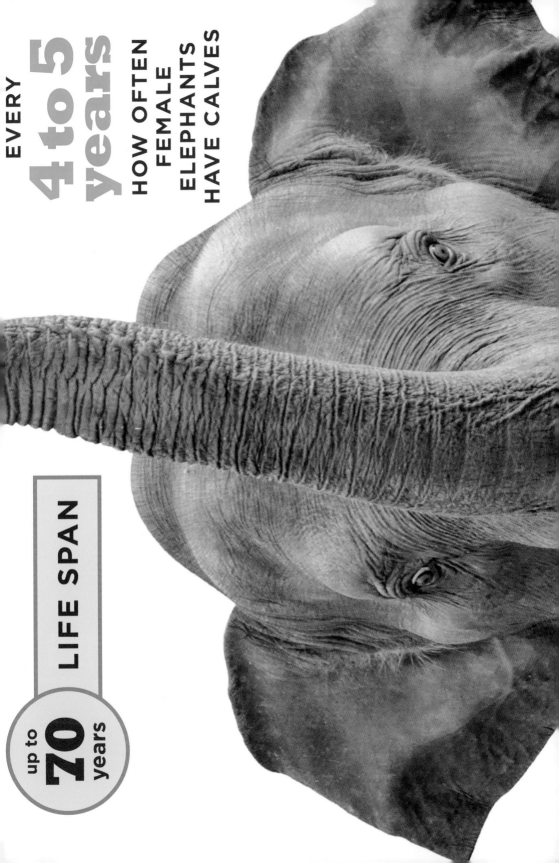

EVERY
**4 to 5
years**

HOW OFTEN
FEMALE
ELEPHANTS
HAVE CALVES

LIFE SPAN

up to **70** years

Baby elephants grow a lot in their first year. They gain about 2 pounds (1 kg) each day. As the years go by, calves keep getting bigger. The young elephants become expert eaters too.

COMPARING SIZES

about
3 FEET
(1 m) tall

7 TO 13 FEET
(2 to 4 m)
tall at shoulder

**NEWBORN
AFRICAN ELEPHANT**

**ADULT
AFRICAN
ELEPHANT**

about
**260
POUNDS**
(118 kg)

**4,409 to 13,889
POUNDS**
(2,000 to 6,300 kg)

Fully Grown

Most elephants are fully grown by their teen years. At 12 to 15 years old, males leave their herds. They join other males or live alone. Females stay with their families. They'll have their own babies someday. But until then, there's a lot of playing and learning to do.

clumsy (KLUHM-zee)—lacking skill or grace in movement

communicate (kuh-MYU-nuh-kayt)—to share information, thoughts, or feelings so they are understood

experienced (ik-SPEER-ee-uhnst)—having skill or knowledge from doing something

nurse (NURS)—to drink milk from the mother's body

predator (PRED-uh-tuhr)—an animal that eats other animals

pregnant (PREG-nuhnt)—carrying one or more unborn offspring in the body

social (SO-shul)—liking to be with and talk to others

sturdy (STUR-dee)—strong and healthy

BOOKS

Best, Arthur. *African Elephants*. Migrating Animals. New York: Cavendish Square, 2019.

Riggs, Kate. *Baby Elephants*. Starting Out. Mankato, MN: Creative Education, 2019.

Terp, Gail. *African Elephants*. Wild Animal Kingdom. Mankato, MN: Black Rabbit Books, 2018.

WEBSITES

African Elephant
kids.sandiegozoo.org/animals/african-elephant

Asian Elephant
kids.nationalgeographic.com/animals/asian-elephant/#three-asian-elephants.jpg

The Elephant
www.ducksters.com/animals/elephant.php

INDEX